AF419942

Elf Secrets

Elf Secrets

Matthew Petchinsky

Elf Secrets: The True Magic of the North Pole
By: Matthew Petchinsky

Introduction: Whispers of the North Pole

Far beyond the frosted peaks and glacial valleys of the Arctic, where the air hums with a chill known only to the stars and ice, lies a realm shrouded in secrecy: the North Pole. This is no ordinary place of snow and solitude. It is a sanctuary of ancient magic, a bastion of light against the encroaching shadows of disbelief and despair. It is here that the legend of Santa Claus finds its heart—and here where whispers speak of those who make the impossible possible: the elves.

To most of the world, the elves are seen as cheerful artisans of merriment, tirelessly crafting toys and trinkets for the delight of children everywhere. Their story is one of simplicity and joy, a tale of busy hands and happy hearts working in harmony. But these tales, delightful as they are, barely scratch the surface of the truth. Beneath the whimsical facade lies an existence far more complex, a tapestry woven with threads of ancient power, sacred duty, and unyielding resolve.

For as long as anyone can remember, the elves have guarded the magic of Christmas, a force far older than Santa Claus himself. This magic is not simply the sparkle of lights or the jingling of bells—it is the lifeblood of hope, generosity, and wonder that pulses through the world during the darkest time of the year. It is an energy drawn from the stars, the earth, and the collective dreams of humanity. And it is the elves who ensure its survival.

Their work is not confined to toy-making. Each elf is a steward of a forgotten art, a bearer of knowledge that stretches back to the dawn of winter itself. From the delicate carving of ice crystals that amplify the auroras, to the intricate weaving of spells that shield the North Pole from prying eyes, their roles are as varied as the stars in the Arctic night. Some elves are engineers of laughter, creating devices to spark joy. Others are guardians of time, ensuring that Santa's journey unfolds without a single hitch. And then there are the Whisperers, those rare few who commune with the ancient forces that govern the balance of light and dark.

But such power comes with a cost, and the elves face challenges few outsiders could fathom. The ever-growing tide of cynicism and commercialism threatens the magic they work so hard to protect. Each year, the barrier between belief and apathy grows thinner, and with it, the magic begins to falter. There are also darker forces—unseen but ever-present—that seek to extinguish the light of Christmas, forces that the elves must confront with courage and cunning.

And yet, they persist. They endure not out of obligation, but out of an unshakable bond with one another and their shared mission. The North Pole is more than a workshop; it is a community, a family, and a fortress. It is a place where ancient wisdom meets modern innovation, where the past and present converge to shape the future. Here, the elves stand as the last line of defense against a world that often forgets how to believe.

In the pages that follow, we will delve deeper into the mysteries of the North Pole and the hidden truths about the elves. You will learn of their origins, their powers, and the extraordinary lengths they go to in order to keep the magic alive. Through their stories, you will come to see Christmas not as a mere holiday, but as a testament to the resilience of wonder and the enduring power of hope.

The North Pole calls to those who dare to dream, to believe, and to seek the extraordinary. The whispers of its secrets beckon. Are you ready to listen?

Chapter 1: The Enchanted Workshop

The heart of the North Pole beats within Santa's Workshop, a sprawling complex unlike anything else on Earth. From the outside, it appears as a whimsical snow-covered castle, its spires shimmering with frost that seems to catch and hold the light of the moon. But within its walls lies a world of unparalleled wonder—a place where the magic of Christmas is brought to life through a combination of ancient enchantments and masterful craftsmanship.

The Rhythm of Magic

Inside the workshop, every corner buzzes with activity. Conveyor belts hum with purpose, carrying brightly colored toys and intricate gadgets through an assembly line that feels almost alive. Machines powered by enchanted crystals glow with warm, golden light as they cut, carve, and polish. The air is thick with the scent of peppermint and cedarwood, mingling with the faint crackle of magic that lingers in every nook and cranny.

The elves move with a rhythm that speaks of centuries of practice. Each one is a specialist, their nimble fingers and sharp minds attuned to their particular craft. Some carve wooden toys with precision that borders on artistry. Others assemble delicate clockwork mechanisms, ensuring every gear and spring fits perfectly. In another corner, a team of elves works tirelessly on the Wish Analyzer, a magical contraption that translates the hopes and dreams of children into a list for Santa's annual journey.

Teamwork is the lifeblood of the workshop. Laughter and chatter fill the air as elves collaborate, solving problems with an ingenuity born of both magic and practicality. They share stories, jokes, and the occasional cup of hot cocoa as they work, their camaraderie as vital to the workshop's success as the tools and spells they wield. Despite the ceaseless workload, their spirits remain high—after all, they are not just making toys; they are weaving joy into every creation.

Meet Tinsel: The Curious Elf

Among the bustling crowd of elves is Tinsel, a young elf with a perpetually inquisitive nature. With her shimmering golden hair tied back with a ribbon and a toolbelt slung over her shoulder, Tinsel is always asking questions, always eager to learn. While others are content to stick to their assigned tasks, Tinsel has a habit of wandering, her curiosity leading her into every corner of the workshop.

This particular morning, Tinsel found herself in the Hall of Archives, a quiet, seldom-visited section of the workshop where records of Christmases past were stored. Massive bookshelves lined the walls, filled with ledgers documenting every toy delivered, every letter received, and every act of kindness rewarded with a gift. Tinsel loved the Archives—not for their history, but for the mysteries they held. She often wondered what secrets lay hidden in their forgotten depths.

The Hidden Room

As Tinsel ran her fingers along the spines of ancient tomes, she noticed something unusual. A faint shimmer of light emanated from behind one of the shelves. Intrigued, she pushed against the shelf, which slid aside with a soft groan to reveal a narrow passageway. Heart racing, she stepped inside.

The hidden room was unlike anything Tinsel had ever seen. The walls were adorned with intricate carvings of the Aurora Borealis, each depiction glowing faintly in the dim light. At the center of the room stood a stone pedestal, upon which rested a collection of scrolls and artifacts. The air felt charged with an ancient energy, as if the room itself was alive.

Tinsel picked up one of the scrolls, unrolling it carefully. The parchment was covered in symbols and diagrams, their meaning unclear at first glance. But as she studied it, a chilling realization began to dawn. The scroll described a powerful connection between the elves' magic and the Aurora Borealis—the radiant dance of lights in the Arctic sky. The scroll spoke of how the auroras served as a conduit for the magic that powered the workshop, infusing the elves with the energy they needed to create and protect the spirit of Christmas.

But there was a problem. Another scroll, written in a hurried hand, revealed that the Aurora Borealis had been dimming over the years. The energy it provided was waning, and with it, the magic of the elves was weakening. If the trend continued, the scroll warned, the workshop would cease to function, and the light of Christmas would flicker and die.

A Chilling Discovery

Tinsel's hands trembled as she read. Her mind raced with questions. Why had no one spoken of this? Did Santa know? And most importantly, what could be done to stop it?

Clutching the scroll, Tinsel hurried back to the main hall of the workshop, her thoughts a whirlwind of concern and determination. She realized that the fading of the auroras was more than just a magical crisis—it was a threat to everything the elves had worked for, everything they believed in. The joy of millions of children depended on their ability to solve this mystery and restore the auroras' brilliance.

As she stepped back into the bustling workshop, the contrast was stark. The elves around her laughed and worked as if nothing was amiss, blissfully unaware of the shadow looming over their world. Tinsel knew she couldn't keep this discovery to herself. But how would they react? Would they believe her? And even if they did, what could they possibly do against such an overwhelming force?

Tinsel took a deep breath, her resolve hardening. She didn't have all the answers, but she knew one thing for certain: she couldn't let the light of Christmas fade. Whatever it took, she would find a way to save the auroras—and with them, the magic of the North Pole.

Little did she know, this was just the beginning of an adventure that would test her courage, challenge her beliefs, and uncover secrets about the North Pole—and herself—that she never imagined.

Chapter 2: The Shard of Aurora

The discovery of the Aurora Borealis' dimming light consumed Tinsel's thoughts. The workshop bustled with its usual cheer, but for Tinsel, the air felt heavier. She couldn't ignore what she'd found—the fading auroras threatened not only their magic but the spirit of Christmas itself. The ancient scroll she'd uncovered hinted at a potential solution: a legendary artifact called the Shard of Aurora.

The Legend of the Shard

The Shard of Aurora, as the scroll recounted, was a crystalline fragment of extraordinary power. Long ago, the elves discovered that the auroras' magic could be amplified through the Shard, a naturally occurring crystal formed at the dawn of time when the first Northern Lights illuminated the Arctic skies. The Shard had become the cornerstone of the elves' magic, enhancing their abilities and ensuring the North Pole remained hidden and protected from the outside world.

But centuries ago, a terrible accident shattered the Shard into countless fragments. The calamity was a result of the elves' own hubris—an attempt to harness the Shard's full power during a particularly dark winter when belief in Christmas was at an all-time low. Though they managed to stabilize the auroras afterward, the Shard's fragments were scattered across the treacherous terrain of the North Pole. Over time, their locations were deliberately obscured to prevent anyone from misusing their power.

Tinsel's heart raced as she read the final line of the scroll: *To restore the Shard of Aurora is to restore the light of hope.*

She knew what she had to do.

Gathering the Team

Tinsel's first stop was to find Jingle, her best friend and partner in all things mischief and adventure. Jingle was as playful as his name suggested, with a shock of silver hair and a knack for inventing gadgets that usually worked—though sometimes a little too well. Tinsel found him in the workshop's Inventorium, tinkering with what appeared to be a jet-powered sled.

"Jingle, I need your help," Tinsel said, her voice urgent. She explained everything she had discovered, from the fading auroras to the legend of the Shard.

Jingle's eyes widened. "The Shard of Aurora? I thought that was just a bedtime story! But if it's real and we can fix it... Well, count me in!"

Their next stop was the library to consult Elder Frost, the oldest and most knowledgeable elf at the North Pole. Elder Frost was a grumpy but wise figure with a flowing white beard and piercing blue eyes that seemed to see straight into your soul. He was a keeper of secrets and had lived through more Christmases than any other elf.

When Tinsel and Jingle explained their mission, Elder Frost listened intently, his expression grim.

"The Shard of Aurora..." he muttered, stroking his beard. "I never thought I'd hear of it again. It is real, young ones, but the quest to recover it is not for the faint of heart. The fragments were hidden in the most perilous corners of the North Pole—places where no elf dares to tread."

"We have to try," Tinsel said, her voice steady. "Without the Shard, the magic of Christmas will fade."

Elder Frost sighed, leaning on his staff. "Very well. I will accompany you. Someone needs to keep you two from freezing or getting eaten by frost wyrms."

The Treacherous Quest Begins

With Elder Frost's reluctant blessing and guidance, the trio prepared for their journey. Tinsel packed her toolbelt with essentials, while Jingle loaded his sled with an assortment of gadgets, including a compass imbued with enchantments to detect magic. Elder Frost, ever the pragmatist, carried a staff carved from enchanted icewood and a satchel of healing potions.

Their first destination was the Crystal Caverns, an underground labyrinth where the first fragment of the Shard was rumored to be hidden. The entrance to the caverns was at the base of Frostfang Mountain, a jagged peak perpetually shrouded in blizzards. As they approached, the temperature plummeted, and the howling wind carried an eerie whisper, as if the mountain itself resented their presence.

Inside the caverns, the air was frigid, and the walls glimmered with veins of ice that reflected their lantern light. The deeper they ventured, the more oppressive the atmosphere became. Strange sounds echoed through the tunnels—scraping, distant growls, and the occasional thud that made them all jump.

The First Fragment

After hours of navigating the maze-like caverns, the trio arrived at a vast chamber. At its center stood a pedestal of ice, and atop it rested the first fragment of the Shard. It was no larger than a child's hand, but it radiated a soft, multicolored glow that bathed the chamber in ethereal light.

Before they could claim it, a roar shook the cavern. From the shadows emerged a Frost Wyrm, a serpentine creature with glistening scales of ice and eyes that burned like cold fire. The creature was a guardian of the Shard, placed there centuries ago to protect it from those unworthy.

Tinsel and Jingle froze in fear, but Elder Frost stepped forward, his staff glowing with magic. "Stand back, young ones. This creature respects strength and wisdom."

Elder Frost engaged the wyrm in a battle of wills, his voice ringing out with ancient incantations. The wyrm roared, its icy breath freezing the ground at their feet, but slowly, it began to back down. Finally, with a final incantation, Elder Frost cast a circle of light around the pedestal, and the wyrm retreated into the shadows.

"You've proven your intent," Elder Frost said, his voice hoarse. "Take the fragment."

Tinsel approached the pedestal with trembling hands and picked up the fragment. As soon as she touched it, she felt a surge of warmth and light, a connection to the auroras that made her heart swell with hope.

"This is only the beginning," Elder Frost warned as they left the cavern. "The other fragments will be harder to find—and harder to claim. But we must press on."

A Spark of Hope

As they emerged from the caverns, the fragment pulsed in Tinsel's hands, its light growing brighter against the dark Arctic sky. For the first time, she felt that their mission was possible. The Shard of Aurora could be restored. The magic of Christmas could be saved.

But deep in her heart, she knew that the challenges ahead would test them in ways they could not yet imagine. The North Pole was full of secrets, and not all of them were friendly.

For now, though, Tinsel allowed herself a small smile. They had taken the first step in a journey that would shape the future of the North Pole—and the world.

Chapter 3: Trials of the Frozen Wilds

The first shard of the Aurora had reignited the group's hope, but Elder Frost's words lingered in the frosty air: "The other fragments will be harder to find—and harder to claim." With the fragment safely tucked into a protective pouch, the trio pressed deeper into the unforgiving expanse of the North Pole, where the frozen wilderness seemed to test their every step.

Their journey was far from ordinary. The North Pole's magical energy was both a blessing and a curse. It shielded the elves from discovery by the outside world but also created pockets of untamed magic, where the land and its creatures were imbued with powers that defied reason. It was in these enchanted, treacherous regions that the remaining shards lay hidden.

The Ice Maze of Whispers

Their first challenge came in the form of the Ice Maze of Whispers, a labyrinth carved from ancient glaciers. The air around the maze shimmered faintly, as if it were alive. Elder Frost explained that the maze had been created by the first generation of elves to guard one of the shards.

"It's said that the maze reflects your fears and doubts," Elder Frost warned. "The whispers are illusions, but they can lead you astray if you let them."

The entrance loomed before them, an archway of jagged ice that seemed to glitter ominously in the pale light. As they stepped inside, the temperature dropped further, and an eerie silence enveloped them. Then came the whispers.

They started softly, faint murmurs at the edge of hearing. But as the group delved deeper into the maze, the voices grew louder, calling each of them by name.

"Tinsel, you're too young for this. Turn back before it's too late."

"Jingle, your inventions always fail. You'll only slow them down."

"Elder Frost, your time has passed. You are weak."

The maze twisted and turned, each corridor looking identical to the last. Tinsel's confidence wavered, and for a moment, she thought about turning back. But then she remembered the fragment glowing in her pouch, a reminder of why they were here.

"Don't listen to them!" she shouted. "The whispers aren't real!"

The others snapped out of their doubt, nodding. Jingle pulled out his enchanted compass, which spun erratically before pointing to the left. Trusting the device, they followed its guidance. The whispers grew louder, but the group's resolve was stronger. At last, they emerged from the maze into a cavern where the second shard glowed atop a pedestal of ice. This time, there was no guardian, only the lingering echoes of their triumph over fear.

"Courage is the foundation of our magic," Elder Frost said as they exited the maze. "Without it, the light of Christmas would fade."

The Mischief of the Frost Sprites

The next shard was hidden in the Glittering Forest, a breathtaking expanse where the trees sparkled with ice crystals, reflecting rainbows of light. It looked like a scene from a snow globe, but Elder Frost warned them to stay vigilant.

"This is the home of the Frost Sprites," he said. "They are mischievous creatures who delight in playing tricks. They won't harm you, but they'll do everything they can to stop you from reaching the shard."

As soon as they stepped into the forest, the Frost Sprites made their presence known. Tiny, translucent figures flitted between the branches, their laughter echoing like the tinkling of bells. At first, their pranks were harmless—snowballs hurled from nowhere and branches shaken to rain down snow. But as the group ventured deeper, the tricks became more elaborate.

Jingle's compass vanished from his hands, reappearing high in a tree. Tinsel's pouch of tools spilled into a snowdrift, and Elder Frost's staff was coated in a layer of sticky frost that refused to melt. The sprites giggled incessantly, darting just out of reach.

Frustrated, Tinsel stopped in her tracks. "We'll never get anywhere if they keep this up!"

Elder Frost raised a hand, his expression thoughtful. "Sprites are creatures of joy. They respond to kindness and fun, not anger."

Tinsel considered his words. Smiling, she pulled a candy cane from her belt and held it aloft. "Would you like a treat?"

The sprites hesitated, their giggles softening into curious murmurs. One brave sprite flitted forward, snatching the candy cane with a tiny, frost-covered hand. The others followed, and soon the group was surrounded by sprites munching on candy and chattering excitedly.

In return for their kindness, the sprites guided the group to a clearing where the third shard rested atop a frozen waterfall. The sprites cleared the path and even provided a rope of enchanted icicles to help Tinsel climb to the top.

"Kindness is another pillar of our magic," Elder Frost said as they left the forest. "Even the smallest act of goodwill can brighten the darkest winter night."

Confronting the Arctic Shadow

The final shard lay in the Abyss of Echoes, a desolate chasm where the Arctic Shadow was said to dwell. The Shadow was a creature born of forgotten holiday wishes, a manifestation of loneliness and despair. It was a being of pure darkness, and Elder Frost warned that it could only be defeated by unwavering belief.

The Abyss was colder and darker than any place they had yet encountered. The air seemed to sap their strength, and even the light from their lanterns struggled to penetrate the gloom. As they descended into the chasm, the Arctic Shadow appeared.

It was an amorphous figure, its form shifting constantly. Eyes like black voids stared at them, and a low growl reverberated through the air. The Shadow's presence was overwhelming, filling them with a deep sense of hopelessness.

"This is impossible," Jingle muttered, his voice trembling. "We'll never beat it."

"No," Tinsel said firmly, stepping forward. "We can."

She reached into her pouch and pulled out the two shards they had already collected. Holding them high, she focused on the belief that had carried them this far—the belief in the magic of Christmas and the power of hope. The shards began to glow, their light pushing back the darkness.

The Shadow roared, its form writhing as the light grew brighter. Tinsel's courage inspired Jingle and Elder Frost, who joined her, each focusing their belief on the shards. The light intensified, and with a final roar, the Arctic Shadow dissolved into nothingness.

At the center of the chasm, they found the final shard, glowing with a light so brilliant it banished the lingering darkness. Together, they had proven that belief—unwavering and true—was the most powerful magic of all.

A Glimmer of Completion

As the group emerged from the Abyss of Echoes, the three shards pulsed in unison, their light mingling to create a vibrant aurora that danced across the sky. They had passed the trials of courage, kindness, and belief, and now held the key to restoring the Shard of Aurora.

But their journey was far from over. The shards needed to be re-forged, a task that would require a level of magic and unity they had yet to master. Still, for the first time, Tinsel felt a glimmer of certainty. Together, they would save the magic of Christmas—and perhaps discover even greater truths about themselves along the way.

Chapter 4: The Aurora Reignited

The journey back to the North Pole was bittersweet. Tinsel, Jingle, and Elder Frost carried the shards of the Aurora safely in their possession, yet they knew their mission was far from complete. The air grew lighter as they neared home, the familiar hum of the North Pole's magic welcoming them back. Still, the group's excitement was tempered by an unspoken tension—they had overcome immense challenges to retrieve the shards, but the most daunting task lay ahead: repairing the Shard of Aurora.

The Great Hall of Lights

The trio stood before the towering doors of the Great Hall of Lights, the most sacred place in the North Pole. Built long before Santa Claus first donned his red suit, the hall was where the auroras were born and where the elves' magic found its source. The massive doors, carved from enchanted ice, were etched with constellations and glowing runes that pulsed faintly, as though sensing the shards' proximity.

Elder Frost stepped forward, placing his hand on the door. The runes flared to life, and with a deep rumble, the doors swung open to reveal a breathtaking sight. The Great Hall was a cavernous chamber of gleaming ice, its walls reflecting every color of the auroras in a dazzling dance of light. At its center stood the Reforging Altar, a circular platform inscribed with intricate symbols and surrounded by floating crystals that resonated with a low, melodic hum.

"This is where it all began," Elder Frost said softly, his voice filled with reverence. "The first elves discovered the auroras here, and it is here that we will reforge the Shard of Aurora."

The Reforging Process

As the group approached the altar, the floating crystals aligned themselves, creating a circle of light around the platform. Tinsel placed the shards carefully on the altar, their multicolored glow reflecting in her wide eyes.

Elder Frost raised his staff, speaking an incantation in the ancient Elvish tongue. The runes on the altar began to glow, and the shards lifted into the air, spinning slowly as beams of light connected them. The shards moved closer together, their jagged edges aligning as if pulled by an invisible force.

But just as the fragments were about to merge, the light faltered. The hum of the crystals grew discordant, and the shards stopped moving. A deep, resonant voice echoed through the hall, ancient and commanding.

"The magic of the auroras is born of selflessness," the voice declared. "To reforge the Shard of Aurora, a sacrifice must be made—something precious, given freely."

A Sacrifice of the Heart

The trio exchanged uneasy glances. Elder Frost frowned, his brow furrowed in thought. Jingle fidgeted nervously, muttering, "What could we possibly offer that's worthy of this magic?"

Tinsel looked down, her mind racing. Her eyes fell on the crystal ornament hanging from her toolbelt, its surface catching the light of the auroras. It was a simple, delicate piece, shaped like a snowflake and infused with a faint inner glow. Her late mentor, an elder elf named Lumin, had given it to her on her first day in the workshop. Lumin had always believed in Tinsel's potential, and the ornament was a symbol of his faith in her.

The thought of parting with it made her chest tighten, but Tinsel knew what had to be done. She unclipped the ornament and held it up, its light mingling with the shards' glow.

"This was a gift from my mentor," she said, her voice steady but tinged with emotion. "It's the most precious thing I own, but I offer it willingly. The magic of Christmas is worth more than any one possession."

The room grew silent as Tinsel placed the ornament on the altar. The floating crystals pulsed, their hum growing harmonious once more. The voice echoed again, softer this time.

"Selflessness is the heart of our magic. Your sacrifice is accepted."

The Shard Reforged

The altar erupted in light as the shards merged into a single, flawless crystal. The Shard of Aurora was whole again, its surface shimmering with all the colors of the Northern Lights. The floating crystals spiraled upward, their combined energy channeled into the shard. A beam of light shot from the shard to the ceiling, piercing through the ice and into the Arctic sky.

Outside, the auroras blazed with renewed brilliance, their colors brighter and more vibrant than ever before. The elves in the workshop and surrounding village paused in their work, gazing upward in awe as the sky came alive with magic.

Tinsel, Jingle, and Elder Frost stood in the Great Hall, their faces illuminated by the shard's glow. Tinsel felt a warmth in her chest, a sense of fulfillment that went beyond words. The loss of her ornament still stung, but she knew it had been the right choice.

A Renewed Spirit

As they left the Great Hall, Tinsel was greeted with cheers and applause. Word of their journey and the successful reforging of the Shard had spread quickly, and the entire North Pole had gathered to celebrate. Santa himself appeared, his eyes twinkling with gratitude.

"You've done something extraordinary," Santa said, placing a hand on Tinsel's shoulder. "The magic of Christmas is stronger than ever, thanks to your courage, kindness, and selflessness."

That night, the North Pole held a grand celebration. The elves danced under the auroras, their laughter echoing through the Arctic.

For the first time in years, the lights felt stronger, as if they had reclaimed the joy and wonder that made them magical.

As the festivities continued, Tinsel stood apart for a moment, gazing at the sky. She felt the presence of her mentor, as if Lumin's faith in her had been carried on the auroras' light. The Shard of Aurora was whole again, but more importantly, the magic of Christmas had been reignited—not just in the North Pole, but in her own heart.

Their journey was complete, but Tinsel knew that the spirit of Christmas required constant care and belief. And as long as she and her fellow elves carried that light within them, the magic would never fade.

Chapter 5: The Magic Within

The North Pole had always been a magical place, but in the days following the reawakening of the Aurora Borealis, it felt more alive than ever before. The vibrant glow of the auroras bathed the snowy landscape in shifting hues of green, blue, and gold, their light reflected in the ice-crusted peaks and shimmering spires of Santa's Workshop. For the first time in years, the elves felt the full strength of their magic, a surge of energy that filled them with purpose and joy.

The North Pole Reborn

The effects of the reawakened auroras were immediate. Machines in the workshop that had begun to slow now hummed with renewed vigor. The Wish Analyzer, once struggling to interpret the dreams of children, now operated with flawless precision. Even the enchanted reindeer stables sparkled with an otherworldly glow as the magical creatures pranced and leaped, eager for their next flight.

The elves themselves were transformed. Their steps were lighter, their laughter louder, and their work filled with a renewed sense of pride and joy. The dull ache of fatigue and doubt that had crept into their lives over the years had been replaced with a boundless energy that could only come from magic restored.

For Tinsel, the changes were deeply personal. As she walked through the workshop, her fellow elves greeted her with gratitude and admiration. To them, she was no longer just a curious young elf with a penchant for wandering; she was a symbol of hope and unity, a reminder of the strength they could find within themselves and each other.

A Lesson for All

Santa called for a gathering in the Great Hall of Lights to commemorate the restoration of the auroras. Every elf in the North Pole gathered in the vast, glowing chamber, their faces illuminated by the dancing lights above. Santa stood at the center of the hall, his presence commanding yet warm, his red coat glistening as though infused with the auroras' light.

Tinsel stood beside him, flanked by Jingle and Elder Frost. Though she was nervous to speak before the crowd, she knew the moment was important.

"Today," Santa began, his deep voice resonating through the hall, "we celebrate more than the restoration of the Shard of Aurora. We celebrate the magic within each of us—the courage, kindness, and belief that make Christmas possible."

He gestured to Tinsel, encouraging her to step forward. Taking a deep breath, she addressed the crowd.

"I've always loved the magic of Christmas," Tinsel said, her voice steady despite her nerves. "But this journey taught me something I never fully understood: our magic isn't just about creating toys or delivering gifts. It's about hope. It's about bringing light to the darkest nights and reminding the world that kindness and belief can overcome anything."

She paused, her gaze sweeping across the crowd. "We all carry that magic within us. It's in the way we work together, the way we care for one another, and the way we keep believing, even when things seem impossible. That's what makes the North Pole so special."

The hall erupted in cheers, the sound echoing off the crystalline walls. Many elves wiped tears from their eyes, moved by Tinsel's heartfelt words.

Keeper of the Aurora

As the cheers subsided, Santa stepped forward once more, his eyes twinkling with pride. "Tinsel, your courage and selflessness have not only restored the Shard of Aurora but reminded us all of what truly matters. It is my honor to name you the Keeper of the Aurora."

A gasp rippled through the crowd. The title was one of great honor and responsibility, bestowed only on those who had shown unparalleled dedication to the magic of the North Pole. As Keeper, Tinsel would be entrusted with ensuring the continued brilliance of the auroras and safeguarding the secrets of the North Pole.

Santa handed Tinsel a staff carved from icewood, its top adorned with a smaller fragment of the Shard of Aurora. The crystal pulsed with light as she took it, a tangible symbol of her new role.

"Tinsel," Santa said, his voice soft but firm, "you have proven yourself a guardian of hope and light. The North Pole is safe because of you, but our work is never truly done. The magic of Christmas must be protected, nurtured, and shared. I trust you to lead us into a future as bright as the auroras themselves."

Tinsel's heart swelled with a mix of pride and humility. "Thank you, Santa. I'll do everything I can to honor this responsibility."

A Bright Future

The celebration continued late into the night, the Great Hall filled with music, dancing, and laughter. Tinsel stood with Jingle and Elder Frost, reflecting on their journey.

"We did it," Jingle said, his silver hair catching the auroras' light. "I mean, *you* did it, Tinsel."

"We all did it," Tinsel replied. "I couldn't have done any of this without you two."

Elder Frost, who rarely smiled, gave her a rare nod of approval. "You've shown wisdom beyond your years, Tinsel. The North Pole is in good hands."

As the festivities wound down, Tinsel found herself gazing at the auroras, their vibrant colors stretching across the Arctic sky. She felt a deep connection to the lights, as though they were a part of her now. Though the journey to restore the Shard of Aurora was complete, she knew it was only the beginning of her adventures as Keeper.

Somewhere out there, she thought, new challenges awaited—forces that might one day threaten the magic of Christmas again. But for now, she allowed herself to bask in the glow of the auroras, their light a testament to the strength of belief, courage, and kindness.

And so, the North Pole thrived once more, its magic renewed, its traditions secure, and its people united. And at the heart of it all stood Tinsel, Keeper of the Aurora, ready to protect the secrets of the North Pole and ensure that the magic of Christmas would shine bright for generations to come.

Appendix A: The History of Elf Magic

The magic of the elves is as ancient as the Arctic winds and as enduring as the stars that guide Santa's sleigh. For millennia, it has been the lifeblood of the North Pole, enabling the elves to fulfill their mission of spreading joy and wonder to the world. This appendix delves into the origins of elf magic, the pivotal role of the Aurora Borealis, the creation of the Shard of Aurora, and the magical hierarchy that ensures its careful stewardship.

1. The Origins of Elf Magic

Elf magic predates even the legend of Santa Claus. It is believed to have originated when the first elves, drawn by the brilliance of the Arctic auroras, settled in the icy wilderness. These early elves discovered that the lights were not merely a natural phenomenon but a powerful source of energy imbued with the essence of hope, kindness, and belief. They named this energy *Aurorite*, and it became the foundation of their magic.

The earliest records, preserved in ancient scrolls housed in the North Pole's Hall of Archives, describe the elves' initial experiments with Aurorite. They learned to harness its power to craft tools, protect their settlement, and eventually create the magical traditions that sustain Christmas. Over time, the elves developed spells, rituals, and artifacts to amplify and channel this energy, leading to the creation of their most significant magical artifact: the Shard of Aurora.

2. The Creation of the Shard of Aurora

The Shard of Aurora was forged during the First Age of Elves, a time when belief in magic was at its strongest. According to legend, the shard was formed from a single crystal of pure Aurorite, extracted from the heart of the Great Hall of Lights. The forging process involved a series of elaborate ceremonies, each requiring the combined efforts of the most skilled elves.

Forging Rituals:

- **The Ceremony of Light:** The first ritual involved capturing the essence of the auroras themselves. Using enchanted mirrors and prisms, the elves redirected the auroras' energy into the crystal, imbuing it with their light.
- **The Binding of Virtues:** The elves infused the crystal with their core values—courage, kindness, and belief—through chants, symbolic offerings, and communal magic.
- **The Final Illumination:** The ritual culminated with the crystal being placed on the Reforging Altar in the Great Hall of Lights, where it absorbed the combined energy of the floating crystals that surrounded it.

The Shard of Aurora became the elves' greatest treasure, amplifying their magic and serving as a conduit between the auroras and the North Pole. It was this artifact that allowed the elves to conceal their home from the outside world, create enchanted toys, and fuel Santa's sleigh on his annual journey.

3. The Aurora Borealis: The Source of Magic

The Aurora Borealis, or Northern Lights, is the wellspring of all elf magic. The lights are believed to be a manifestation of the world's collective hope, generosity, and wonder. They grow brighter when belief in Christmas is strong and dimmer when doubt or cynicism takes hold.

The Aurora's Functions:

1. **Magical Energy:** The auroras emit Aurorite, the energy that fuels the elves' magic. This energy flows through the Great Hall of Lights, where it is distributed throughout the North Pole.
2. **Protection:** The auroras create a magical barrier that shields the North Pole from detection by the outside world.
3. **Inspiration:** The lights serve as a symbol of hope and wonder, reminding the elves of their purpose.

4. The Magical Hierarchy of the North Pole

Elf society is structured around the careful management and application of magic. The hierarchy ensures that every aspect of life in the North Pole operates in harmony.

Key Roles:

1. **The Keeper of the Aurora:** The highest magical authority, responsible for safeguarding the Shard of Aurora and ensuring the continued brilliance of the auroras. This role is currently held by Tinsel.
2. **The Elders' Council:** A group of the oldest and wisest elves, including Elder Frost, who oversee the preservation of ancient knowledge and traditions.
3. **The Artisans:** These elves specialize in crafting enchanted toys, tools, and artifacts, combining magic and craftsmanship.
4. **The Whisperers:** A rare group of elves capable of communicating directly with the auroras to interpret their messages and predict changes in their energy.
5. **The Guardians:** Tasked with protecting the North Pole from external threats, both magical and mundane.

5. The Great Hall of Lights

The Great Hall of Lights is the epicenter of elf magic and the most sacred location in the North Pole. It is here that the auroras' energy is harnessed and where major ceremonies, such as the reforging of the Shard of Aurora, are performed.

Structure of the Hall:

- **The Reforging Altar:** Located at the center of the hall, the altar is a circular platform inscribed with ancient runes. It is surrounded by floating crystals that channel and amplify magical energy.
- **The Crystalline Walls:** The hall's walls are made of enchanted ice that reflects and magnifies the light of the auroras.
- **The Celestial Dome:** The ceiling is transparent, allowing the auroras to be seen directly from within the hall.

(Diagram of the Great Hall of Lights included here)

6. Magical Symbols and Their Meanings

The elves use a system of runes and symbols in their ceremonies and artifacts. These symbols are carved into tools, woven into clothing, and etched into the walls of the Great Hall of Lights.

Key Symbols:

- **Rune of Light:** Represents the power of the auroras and is used in rituals involving illumination and clarity.
- **Rune of Unity:** Symbolizes the bond between elves and is engraved on the Reforging Altar.
- **Rune of Hope:** A central symbol in the Ceremony of Light, signifying the essence of Christmas magic.
- **Rune of Protection:** Found on the enchanted barriers surrounding the North Pole.

(Diagram of magical symbols with detailed descriptions included here)

Conclusion

The history of elf magic is a testament to the resilience and ingenuity of the North Pole's inhabitants. From the origins of Aurorite to the creation of the Shard of Aurora and the magical hierarchy that sustains their way of life, the elves' story is one of unity, courage, and unwavering belief. As the Keeper of the Aurora, Tinsel now carries this legacy forward, ensuring that the magic of Christmas continues to shine brightly for generations to come.

Appendix B: Creatures and Mysteries of the North Pole

The North Pole is a land of unparalleled magic and wonder, teeming with creatures both enchanting and mysterious. These beings, shaped by the unique energy of the Aurora Borealis, play a vital role in the balance of this magical realm. This appendix explores the Frost Sprites, the Arctic Shadow, and other extraordinary creatures encountered during Tinsel's journey, offering insights into their behavior, origins, and how to interact with them. For those brave enough to navigate the Frozen Wilds, practical tips are also included to ensure your safety and success.

1. Frost Sprites

Guardians of the Glittering Forest

Description:

Frost Sprites are small, ethereal beings with translucent, shimmering bodies that reflect the colors of the auroras. Standing no taller than a snow globe, they have delicate wings that resemble frost-covered leaves and emit a faint, bell-like chime as they move. Their laughter is melodic, often heard before they are seen.

Behavior:

Frost Sprites are playful and mischievous, delighting in harmless tricks like hiding objects, creating small snow flurries, and redirecting travelers. Despite their pranks, they are not malicious and can be won over with acts of kindness or offerings of sweets, particularly peppermint.

Fun Facts:

- Frost Sprites have a natural affinity for creating intricate ice sculptures, often leaving behind frozen masterpieces that sparkle in the morning light.
- They are believed to help nurture the Glittering Forest by spreading magical frost that enhances the beauty and strength of the trees.

Tips for Adventurers:

- **Carry candy or shiny trinkets:** These can distract or befriend the sprites if they become too playful.
- **Speak kindly:** Sprites respond positively to gentle words and laughter.
- **Follow their trails:** If befriended, Frost Sprites will guide you safely through the forest.

2. The Arctic Shadow

The Guardian of the Abyss of Echoes

Description:

The Arctic Shadow is a massive, amorphous creature formed of pure darkness, with shifting tendrils and glowing void-like eyes. It is a manifestation of forgotten holiday wishes, despair, and loneliness. Despite its fearsome appearance, the Shadow is not inherently evil but exists as a reminder of the consequences of losing hope.

Behavior:

The Arctic Shadow resides deep in the Abyss of Echoes, where it guards the fragile balance of light and dark in the North Pole. It confronts intruders with waves of despair and fear, testing their resolve and belief. The Shadow can only be defeated or pacified by unwavering courage and the light of selfless magic.

Fun Facts:

- The Arctic Shadow's form shifts based on the fears of those who encounter it, making it unique to each observer.
- Legends say the Shadow can transform into a benevolent guide if presented with a symbol of pure hope, such as a heartfelt wish or act of kindness.

Tips for Adventurers:

- **Stay together:** The Shadow preys on isolation and fear.
- **Carry a light source:** Magical lanterns imbued with aurora energy can repel its darkness.
- **Focus on hope:** Reciting positive memories or wishes can weaken its influence.

3. Frost Wyrms

Guardians of the Ice Caverns

Description:

Frost Wyrms are serpentine creatures with crystalline scales that sparkle like diamonds. They have icy blue eyes and wings made of translucent ice, enabling them to glide silently through the caverns they protect. Frost Wyrms are ancient creatures, deeply tied to the magical energy of the auroras.

Behavior:

Frost Wyrms are fiercely territorial and act as guardians of sacred places, such as the Ice Caverns where shards of the Aurora are often hidden. They are intelligent and respect strength and wisdom, often testing intruders before allowing passage.

Fun Facts:

- Their breath can freeze anything in its path, creating sculptures of ice that remain for centuries.
- Frost Wyrms are said to sing in the presence of strong aurora energy, their deep, resonant tones echoing through the caverns.

Tips for Adventurers:

- **Avoid sudden movements:** Approach Frost Wyrms calmly and respectfully.
- **Carry enchanted items:** A staff or talisman infused with aurora magic can help establish trust.
- **Be prepared for riddles:** Some wyrms are known to test travelers with puzzles or challenges.

4. Snowlight Owls

Messengers of the North Pole

Description:

Snowlight Owls are large, majestic birds with pure white feathers that shimmer faintly in the moonlight. Their eyes glow softly, and their hoots sound like distant wind chimes. These owls are highly intelligent and are often used as messengers between the elves.

Behavior:

Snowlight Owls are loyal and reliable, known for their ability to navigate even the fiercest blizzards. They bond closely with their handlers and can sense emotions, often comforting those in distress with their calming presence.

Fun Facts:

- Snowlight Owls' feathers are said to bring good luck when carried as charms.
- They can understand Elvish commands and are often seen delivering scrolls or packages throughout the North Pole.

Tips for Adventurers:

- **Respect their space:** Snowlight Owls are proud creatures and appreciate gentle handling.
- **Carry a token of trust:** Offering a small enchanted gift can establish a bond.
- **Follow their flight paths:** Owls often know the safest routes through the Frozen Wilds.

5. Ice Wisps

Ethereal Spirits of the Frozen Wilds

Description:

Ice Wisps are small, glowing orbs of light that float aimlessly through the tundra. They leave trails of frost in their wake and emit a soft, chiming hum. These elusive beings are said to be fragments of the auroras given form.

Behavior:

Ice Wisps are harmless and curious, often following travelers for short distances. They are drawn to warmth and kindness and are believed to bring good fortune to those they linger near.

Fun Facts:

- Ice Wisps are known to lead lost travelers to safety, though their intentions are never explicitly clear.
- They are attracted to music, often appearing near singing elves or the sound of bells.

Tips for Adventurers:

- **Do not chase them:** Wisps cannot be caught and will vanish if pursued too aggressively.
- **Sing softly:** A gentle melody can encourage a wisp to guide you.
- **Follow their trails:** The frost patterns they leave often point toward hidden paths.

Conclusion

The creatures and mysteries of the North Pole are as diverse and magical as the auroras themselves. While some may pose challenges, they are all integral to the balance and beauty of this enchanted realm. For those who venture into the Frozen Wilds, remember: kindness, courage, and respect for the magic of the North Pole are the keys to success. Let the auroras guide your path, and may your journey be filled with wonder.

<u>Message from the Author:</u>

I hope you enjoyed this book, I love astrology and knew there was not a book such as this out on the shelf. I love metaphysical items as well. Please check out my other books:

-Life of Government Benefits

-My life of Hell

-My life with Hydrocephalus

-Red Sky

-World Domination:Woman's rule

-World Domination:Woman's Rule 2: The War

-Life and Banishment of Apophis: book 1

-The Kidney Friendly Diet

-The Ultimate Hemp Cookbook

-Creating a Dispensary(legally)

-Cleanliness throughout life: the importance of showering from childhood to adulthood.

-Strong Roots: The Risks of Overcoddling children

-Hemp Horoscopes: Cosmic Insights and Earthly Healing

- Celestial Hemp Navigating the Zodiac: Through the Green Cosmos

-Astrological Hemp: Aligning The Stars with Earth's Ancient Herb

-The Astrological Guide to Hemp: Stars, Signs, and Sacred Leaves

-Green Growth: Innovative Marketing Strategies for your Hemp Products and Dispensary

-Cosmic Cannabis

-Astrological Munchies

-Henry The Hemp

-Zodiacal Roots: The Astrological Soul Of Hemp

- **Green Constellations: Intersection of Hemp and Zodiac**

-Hemp in The Houses: An astrological Adventure Through The Cannabis Galaxy

-Galactic Ganja Guide

Heavenly Hemp

Zodiac Leaves

Doctor Who Astrology

Cannastrology

Stellar Satvias and Cosmic Indicas

<u>Celestial Cannabis: A Zodiac Journey</u>

AstroHerbology: The Sky and The Soil: Volume 1

AstroHerbology:Celestial Cannabis:Volume 2

Cosmic Cannabis Cultivation

The Starry Guide to Herbal Harmony: Volume 1

The Starry Guide to Herbal Harmony: Cannabis Universe: Volume 2

Yugioh Astrology: Astrological Guide to Deck, Duels and more

Nightmare Mansion: Echoes of The Abyss

Nightmare Mansion 2: Legacy of Shadows

Nightmare Mansion 3: Shadows of the Forgotten

Nightmare Mansion 4: Echoes of the Damned

The Life and Banishment of Apophis: Book 2

Nightmare Mansion: Halls of Despair

<u>Healing with Herb: Cannabis and Hydrocephalus</u>

<u>Planetary Pot: Aligning with Astrological Herbs: Volume 1</u>

Fast Track to Freedom: 30 Days to Financial Independence Using AI, Assets, and Agile Hustles

<u>Cosmic Hemp Pathways</u>

How to Become Financially Free in 30 Days: 10,000 Paths to Prosperity

Zodiacal Herbage: Astrological Insights: Volume 1

Nightmare Mansion: Whispers in the Walls
The Daleks Invade Atlantis
Henry the hemp and Hydrocephalus

10X The Kidney Friendly Diet
Cannabis Universe: Adult coloring book
Hemp Astrology: The Healing Power of the Stars
Zodiacal Herbage: Astrological Insights: Cannabis Universe: Volume 2
<u>Planetary Pot: Aligning with Astrological Herbs: Cannabis Universes: Volume 2</u>
Doctor Who Meets the Replicators and SG-1: The Ultimate Battle for Survival
Nightmare Mansion: Curse of the Blood Moon
<u>The Celestial Stoner: A Guide to the Zodiac</u>
Cosmic Pleasures: Sex Toy Astrology for Every Sign
Hydrocephalus Astrology: Navigating the Stars and Healing Waters
Lapis and the Mischievous Chocolate Bar

Celestial Positions: Sexual Astrology for Every Sign
Apophis's Shadow Work Journal: **:** A Journey of Self-Discovery and Healing
Kinky Cosmos: Sexual Kink Astrology for Every Sign
Digital Cosmos: The Astrological Digimon Compendium
Stellar Seeds: The Cosmic Guide to Growing with Astrology
Apophis's Daily Gratitude Journal

Cat Astrology: Feline Mysteries of the Cosmos
The Cosmic Kama Sutra: An Astrological Guide to Sexual Positions
Unleash Your Potential: A Guided Journal Powered by AI Insights
Whispers of the Enchanted Grove

Cosmic Pleasures: An Astrological Guide to Sexual Kinks

369, 12 Manifestation Journal

Whisper of the nocturne journal(blank journal for writing or drawing)

The Boogey Book

Locked In Reflection: A Chastity Journey Through Locktober

Generating Wealth Quickly:

How to Generate $100,000 in 24 Hours

Star Magic: Harness the Power of the Universe

The Flatulence Chronicles: A Fart Journal for Self-Discovery

The Doctor and The Death Moth

Seize the Day: A Personal Seizure Tracking Journal

The Ultimate Boogeyman Safari: A Journey into the Boogie World and Beyond

Whispers of Samhain: 1,000 Spells of Love, Luck, and Lunar Magic: Samhain Spell Book

Apophis's guides:

Witch's Spellbook Crafting Guide for Halloween

<u>Frost & Flame: The Enchanted Yule Grimoire of 1000 Winter Spells</u>

<u>The Ultimate Boogey Goo Guide & Spooky Activities for Halloween Fun</u>

Harmony of the Scales: A Libra's Spellcraft for Balance and Beauty

The Enchanted Advent: 36 Days of Christmas Wonders

Nightmare Mansion: The Labyrinth of Screams

Harvest of Enchantment: 1,000 Spells of Gratitude, Love, and Fortune for Thanksgiving

The Boogey Chronicles: A Journal of Nightly Encounters and Shadowy Secrets

The 12 Days of Financial Freedom: A Step-by-Step Christmas Countdown to Transform Your Finances

The Ultimate Black Friday Prepper's Guide: Mastering Shopping Strategies and Savings

Cosmic Sales: The Astrological Guide to Black Friday Shopping

Legends of the Corn Mother and Other Harvest Myths

Whispers of the Harvest: The Corn Mother's Journal

The Evergreen Spellbook

The Doctor Meets the Boogeyman

The White Witch of Rose Hall's SpellBook

The Gingerbread Golem's Shadow: A Study in Sweet Darkness

The Gingerbread Golem Codex: An Academic Exploration of Sweet Myths

The Gingerbread Golem Grimoire: Sweet Magicks and Spells for the Festive Witch

The Curse of the Gingerbread Golem

10-minute Christmas Crafts for kids

<u>Christmas Crisis Solutions: The Ultimate Last-Minute Survival Guide</u>

Gingerbread Golem Recipes: Holiday Treats with a Magical Twist

The Infinite Key: Unlocking Mystical Secrets of the Ages

Enchanted Yule: A Wiccan and Pagan Guide to a Magical and Memorable Season

Dinosaurs of Power: Unlocking Ancient Magick

Astro-Dinos: The Cosmic Guide to Prehistoric Wisdom

Gallifrey's Yule Logs: A Festive Doctor Who Cookbook

The Dino Grimoire: Secrets of Prehistoric Magick

The Gift They Never Knew They Needed

The Gingerbread Golem's Culinary Alchemy: Enchanting Recipes for a Sweetly Dark Feast

A Time Lord Christmas: Holiday Adventures with the Doctor

Krampusproofing Your Home: Defensive Strategies for Yule

Silent Frights: A Collection of Christmas Creepypastas to Chill Your Bones

Santa Raptor's Jolly Carnage: A Dino-Claus Christmas Tale

Prehistoric Palettes: A Dino Wicca Coloring Journey
The Christmas Wishkeeper Chronicles
The Starlight Sleigh: A Holiday Journey
If you want solar for your home go here: https://www.harborso-lar.live/apophisenterprises/

Get Some Tarot cards: https://www.makeplayingcards.com/sell/apophis-occult-shop

Get some shirts: https://www.bonfire.com/store/apophis-shirt-emporium/

<u>Instagrams:</u>
@apophis_enterprises,
@apophisbookemporium,
@apophisscardshop
Twitter: @apophisenterpr1
Tiktok:@apophisenterprise
Youtube: @sg1fan23477, @FiresideRetreatKingdom
Hive: @sg1fan23477
CheeLee: @SG1fan23477

Podcast: Apophis Chat Zone: https://open.spotify.com/show/5zXbrCLEV2xzCp8ybrfHsk?si=fb4d4fdbdce44dec

Newsletter: https://apophiss-newsletter-27c897.beehiiv.com/

If you want to support me or see posts of other projects that I have come over to: **buymeacoffee.com/mpetchinskg**
I post there daily several times a day

Get your Dinowicca or Christmas themed digital products, especially Santa Raptor songs and other musics. Here: **https://sg1fan23477.gumroad.com**

Apophis Yuletide Digital has not only digital Christmas items, but it will have all things with Dinowicca as well as other Digital products.

www.ingramcontent.com/pod-product-compliance
Lightning Source LLC
Chambersburg PA
CBHW061724130726
47996CB00006B/2490